Peas let her be a Princess

by Diane E. Keyes

Illustrated by Hannah Mericle

Puddle Press

Publisher's Cataloging-in-Publication Data
provided by Five Rainbows Services

Keyes, Diane E.
   Peas let her be a princess / Diane E. Keyes ; illustrations
by Hannah Mericle.
   pages cm
  ISBN: 978-0-9962098-0-9 (hardcover)
  ISBN: 978-0-9962098-2-3 (pbk.)
  ISBN: 978-0-9962098-1-6 (e-book)
  1. Princesses—Fiction. 2. Perseverance
(Ethics)—Fiction. 3. Fairy tales. 4. Humorous stories.
5. Stories in rhyme.   I. Mericle, Hannah, illustrator. II.
Title.
PZ7.1.K49 Pe 2015
[Fic]—dc23

2015941714
Printed in the United States of America
First Edition
10 9 8 7 6 5 4 3 2 1
Published by Puddle Press
62 Hillcrest Street, Oviedo, FL 32765
puddle.press@gmail.com
www.thelitalliance.org

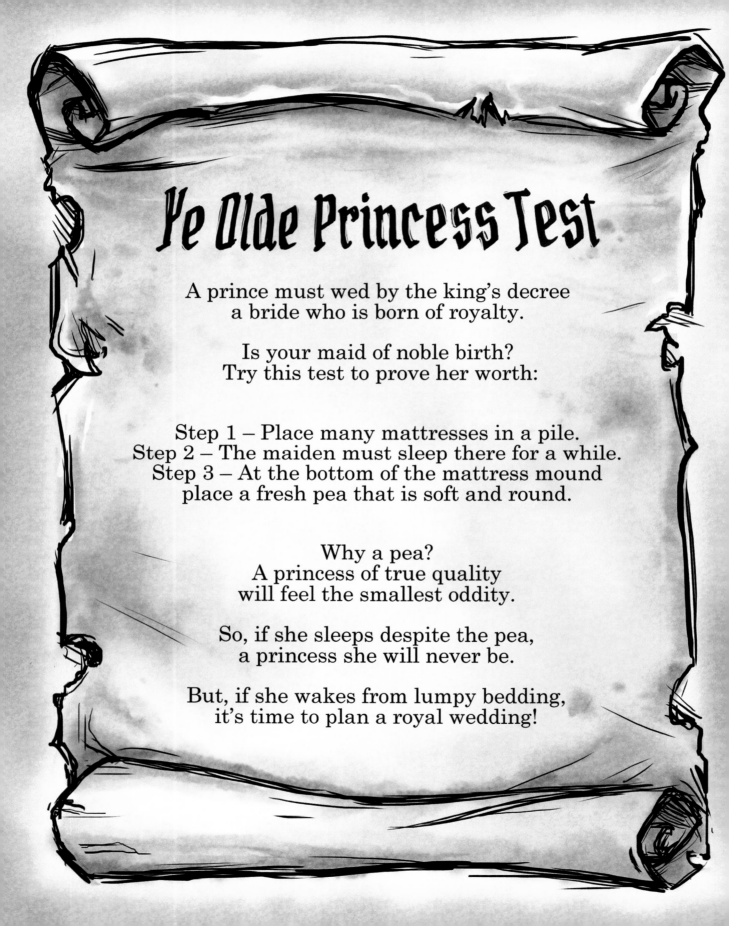

Ye Olde Princess Test

A prince must wed by the king's decree
a bride who is born of royalty.

Is your maid of noble birth?
Try this test to prove her worth:

Step 1 – Place many mattresses in a pile.
Step 2 – The maiden must sleep there for a while.
Step 3 – At the bottom of the mattress mound
place a fresh pea that is soft and round.

Why a pea?
A princess of true quality
will feel the smallest oddity.

So, if she sleeps despite the pea,
a princess she will never be.

But, if she wakes from lumpy bedding,
it's time to plan a royal wedding!

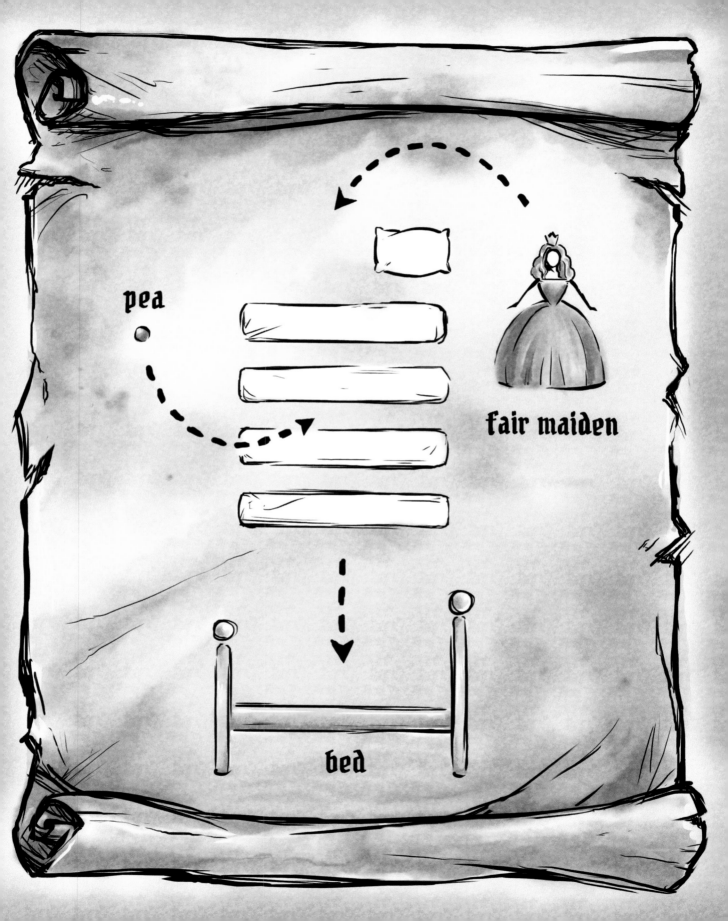

pea

fair maiden

bed

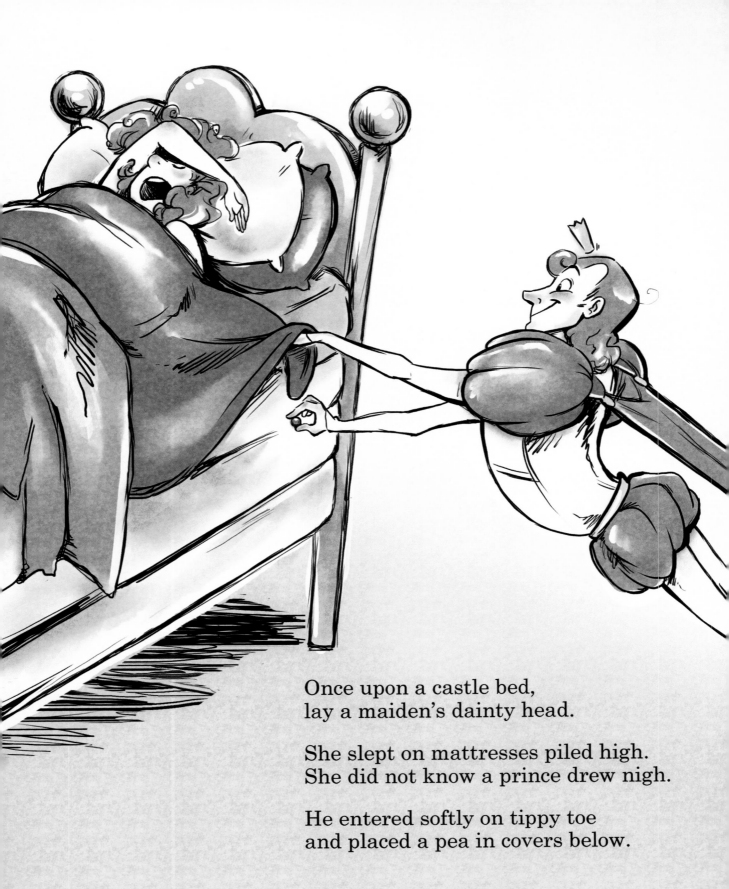

Once upon a castle bed,
lay a maiden's dainty head.

She slept on mattresses piled high.
She did not know a prince drew nigh.

He entered softly on tippy toe
and placed a pea in covers below.

Behind him crept his loyal knight,
ready to guard, protect, and fight.

A hungry mouse spied the pea,
"A perfect snack, just for me!"

The prince roared, "Halt, marauding mouse.
That pea is for my future spouse."

The brave knight advanced, "Rat, fear my sword!"
"No need for violence," the mouse implored.

"You seem upset
and rather frayed.
But I can help,
put down your blade.

You think a pea beneath the bed
proves her a princess you can wed?"

The prince sneered, "Yes, you pilfering pest!
My love must pass the Princess Test."

The young maid's snore shook the air,
startling the royal heir.

He jumped into the knight's embrace.
Searched for the noise that filled the space.

Then he slumped, "My love has failed the test."
The mouse inquired, "May I suggest?

A pea is really quite petite!
Try something bigger, more concrete.

Add some cheddar, a big hunk of cheese!
Your maiden will feel that lump with ease."

The prince considered the odd advice.
Then he nodded, "Knight, get me a slice."

The knight pushed in the tasty treat.
The prince crossed fingers, hands, and feet.

"Cunning critter, I hope you're right.
Do her eyes open? No! Not quite."

Unperturbed, the mouse concentrated.
Then winked and grinned and boldly stated,

"A melon! That's a better test.
Your gal will rouse, she will not rest."

The damsel snuffled, scratched her nose,
shifted—but continued to doze.

Bemoaned the prince, "She does not wake."
The mouse squeaked, "Get a frosted cake!"

The prince shoved and pushed the cake within.
She slumbered on, making quite a din.

The mouse squealed,
"A sheep beneath the sheets!
Its curly wool, its hooves,
and bleats . . .

. . . will surely waken the maiden now!
She does not stir? How about a cow!"

It mooed and snorted in the air.
"Still, she sleeps?" the mouse screeched.

"A bear!"

The bear was stuffed into the bed.
It pawed and roared quite near her head.

The maiden woke. She sat up straight.
"Quieeeeettttt!" she bellowed quite irate.

"I've barely gotten any sleep.
I am so tired I could weep.

I felt a pea, a melon, a cake,
some cheese, a barnyard for goodness sake!"

All at once there was a crack.
Trembling the mattress stack.

The animals shook, shivered, shifted.
The young maid teetered, tottered, twisted.

They tumbled, falling from the bed
tossing the maiden on her head.

"She passed the test!" the mouse did cheer.
"Prince, grab your bride and pull her near."

The prince gushed, "We'll have eternal bliss.
Let's seal the deal with a little kiss!"

The princess yelped. Her eyes grew wide.
She squared her shoulders and replied,

"Live here with beds like this? No way!
I'd rather sleep on straw and hay."

And so she left. The poor prince sighed,
"My love is gone!" And then he cried!

The cow, the sheep, the bear looked on.
Perplexed to find the princess gone.

"This is awkward."

"And quite unseemly."

"Does the prince get
snubbed this routinely?"

But fairy tales don't end this way.
We know she turned around to . . .

"Wait, were you about to say 'stay'? No way!

My back is really very sore.
I'll sleep on lumpy beds no more!"

She left for good. The mouse groaned, "Oh dear."
Then he wiped away a princely tear.

"Do not fret that this did not go well.
What if, next time, we use a gazelle?"

The sad prince gave his nose a blow.
But then a smile began to grow.

"Regal rodent, I must agree!
Its pointy horns and knobby knees.

But what about a platypus?
Or better yet, an octopus!"

And now our story has reached its end.
Of a pea, a prince, and his new best friend.

"The maid moooooved on.
She's outta here."

"Stuffing the bed was baaaaad,
that's clear."

"But, our Prince is
beeaaring it well."

"So let's eat cake.
Good niighhtttt, farewell."

The End

Diane E. Keyes was born in Gainesville, FL. She received undergraduate degrees in Art and English from Principia College and a MLIS from the University of South Florida. She is the president and founder of The Literacy Alliance, a Central Florida nonprofit (see below), a Youth Services Librarian for her nearby county library, and the mother of three. Diane lives with her husband, two dogs, and two cats in sunny Florida. *Peas let her be a Princess*, (Puddle Press, 2015) is her first published children's book.

Hannah Mericle is the recipient of a Bachelors degree in Illustration from The Art Institute of Fort Lauderdale, and resides in Central Florida where she spends the majority of her days being creative. She receives constant love and support from her husband and sometimes from her pet chinchilla. She is a Visual Artist and Designer for a local chocolate factory, a Freelance Illustrator, and an avid supporter of art programs for kids and teens. *Peas let her be a Princess*, (Puddle Press, 2015) is the third book Hannah has illustrated and the first one to be formally published.

The Literacy Alliance

10% of sale proceeds from this book will be donated to The Literacy Alliance. The Literacy Alliance strives to make a positive difference in the lives of teenagers and children by encouraging them to discover the rewards and joy of reading.

For more information check out their website at http://thelitalliance.org. Like them on Facebook, follow them on YouTube, Twitter, Pinterest, and Instagram.